Dear mouse friends,
Welcome to the world of

Geronimo Stilton

THE RODENT'S GAZETTE
EDITORIAL STAFF

Geronimo Stilton
A learned and brainy
mouse; editor of
The Rodent's Gazette

Thea Stilton
Geronimo's sister and
special correspondent at
The Rodent's Gazette

Trap Stilton
An awful joker;
Geronimo's cousin and
owner of the store
Cheap Junk for Less

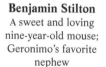

Benjamin Stilton
A sweet and loving
nine-year-old mouse;
Geronimo's favorite
nephew

Geronimo Stilton

THE MYSTERIOUS CHEESE THIEF

Scholastic Inc.

New York   Toronto   London   Auckland   Sydney

Mexico City   New Delhi   Hong Kong   Buenos Aires

ISBN 978-0-439-02312-2

www.geronimostilton.com

Published by Scholastic Inc., 557 Broadway, New York, NY 10012. SCHOLASTIC and associated logos are trademarks and/or registered trademarks of Scholastic Inc.

Text by Geronimo Stilton
Original title Il misterioso ladro di formaggi
Cover by Lorenzo Chiavini and Giuseppe Ferrario
Illustrations by Silvia Bigolin, Mirella Monesi, Maria DeFilippio, and Valentina Grassini
Graphics by Merenguita Gingermouse

Special thanks to Kathryn Cristaldi
Interior design by Kay Petronio

27   18 19 20/0

Printed in the U.S.A.   40
First printing, August 2007

Geronimo Stilton

I'M PROUD OF
MY NAME!

Hello, mouse fans. Have we met? My name is Stilton, *Geronimo Stilton*. Did you know that Stilton is the name of a very special cheese that is made in England? I didn't.

But then I went on a trip in my grandfather's cheese-colored camper. I found out lots of things I never knew about cheeses, and, more importantly, about my family. It all started like this . . .

Geronimo Stilton
PUBLISHER OF *THE RODENT'S GAZETTE*,
THE MOST FAMOUS NEWSPAPER ON
MOUSE ISLAND

ARE YOU SURE YOUR NAME IS STILTON?

It was a **freezing-cold** Friday night in winter. I should have been home warming my paws by the fire, but I wasn't. Instead, I was working late at the office, putting together an illustrated encyclopedia of cheeses. I was just drooling over a photograph of some cheddar cheese balls when the bell rang.

Ding-dong! Ding-dong!

At the door stood a distinguished-looking **rodent**. He was dressed in a very expensive suit and carried a thick **FOLDER** filled with papers.

"Good evening," he squeaked. "I'm looking for the mouse who calls himself Geronimo STILTON."

"I'm the mouse, I mean the Stilton, er, that is — I'm *Geronimo Stilton*," I stammered. Then I stuck out my paw. Aunt Sweetfur always told me that a pawshake is the *polite* way to greet a visitor.

But the rodent just scowled. I guess he missed that lesson on manners.

"STILTON?" he replied in a snide voice. "You mean STILTON, starting with an 's' and ending with an 'n'? Are you certain that's really your name?"

I puffed up my fur. Who did this **rude** mouse think he was?

"Of course, I'm sure my name is STILTON!"

I insisted. "I've been a STILTON since the day I was born. It's my family name."

The mouse just *smirked*. Then he handed me an official-looking piece of paper.

"I wouldn't be **so sure** about that," he said. Then, without another word, he turned and left.

BAFFLED, I closed the door behind him.

What a strange visitor. Then I thought of something. Maybe he was from that crazy reality TV show, *Say Squeak!* I looked around my office for hidden cameras. Was someone playing a *trick* on me?

Maybe the document in my paw would help me get to the bottom of this. I cleaned my glasses, so I could see better. Then I began to read.

The paper was from the well-known rodent lawyer Ratly Von Doright III.

It said:

Dear Mr. Geronimo:

We are writing to inform you that from this day forward you may no longer use the last name Stilton to refer to yourself or any other member of your family.

Obviously, you are not aware that the name Stilton is the registered trademark of an English cheese. (And not just any cheese—Stilton is the king of English cheeses!)

Therefore, you must cease and desist using this name immediately, or we will be forced to take further action!

Yours cheesily,
Ratly Von Doright III Esq.
Counsel to the Stilton Cheesemakers' Association

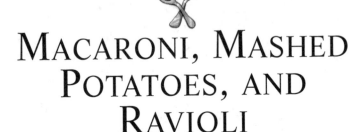

MACARONI, MASHED POTATOES, AND RAVIOLI

I was more baffled then ever.

I decided to go straight home.

The sun was setting over New Mouse City. It reminded me of a tasty slice of orange cheddar. My tummy grumbled. I felt like I hadn't eaten in weeks, months, years. Well, OK, maybe it was just since lunch.

Still, I was starving.

At last, I arrived home. I lit a **COZY** fire in the **FIREPLACE**.

Then I raced to the kitchen.

In a flash, I whipped up my dinner: a creamy plate of macaroni and cheese, a bowl of mozzarella mashed potatoes, a pan of cheese ravioli, **CHEDDAR ROLLS**, and a triple-decker cheesecake for dessert.

OK, maybe I overdid it with the cheese-cake. But can you blame a starving mouse?

As I was cooking, I decided to call my sister, Thea. I told her about the **strange** letter from England.

"Not allowed to use the name STILTON!" she exclaimed. "I'll be over right away. *What are you making for dinner?*"

Before I could reply, she hung up.

A few minutes later, the doorbell rang. It was Thea and my little nephew Benjamin.

"Uncle Geronimo, May I Have Dinner with you, too?" Benjamin squeaked when I answered the door.

He wrapped his little paws around me in a mouse-size hug.

How could I say no?

I had just set out two more plates when the doorbell rang again. This time it was my obnoxious cousin Trap.

"Hello there, Germeister. I'm here for the family reunion! Get out the grub. This mouse is famished!" he announced.

"Reunion?" I mumbled.

But Trap wasn't listening. He pushed me aside and marched into the kitchen. Then he began tasting everything in sight.

"Hmm, this macaroni and cheese needs more milk. It's as dry as Great-Grandfather Sandysnout's whiskers," he snickered.

I was fuming.

Of course, my cousin didn't notice. He squeaked on and on about the lumpy mashed potatoes, the rock-hard cheddar rolls, and the soupy cheesecake.

"Did I mention I'm taking a course to become a cheeseologist, Gerry Berry? That means I'll be an expert on all things cheesy," he boasted.

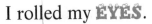
I rolled my EYES.

I was about to explain that there is no such thing as a cheeseologist when the phone rang.

It was my grandfather **William Shortpaws**.

"Grandson! What's this I hear about the letter you received regarding the family name?! How dare they tell us to change it? How ridiculous! How unmousely!" he ranted. "I'll be over in two minutes!"

"But, Grandfather . . ." I began.

Of course, he had already hung up. Oh, why does no one ever listen to me? I'm a good mouse. I brush between meals. I cross on the green and not in between. I cover my snout when I *SNEEZE*. Well, except for that one time. But I had been really sick. I had the flu. I could barely reach my nightstand to get a tissue.

FAMILY REUNION

I was still thinking about the flu when Grandfather William arrived. He was accompanied by his housekeeper, Tina Spicytail. Actually, Tina is not just Grandfather's housekeeper. She also keeps *him* in line!

I was about to close the door again when I heard **shouting**. Outside, all of my relatives had gathered on my front stoop. I glared at my cousin Trap. It looked like

someone had spread the word about our so-called "family reunion."

Within minutes, a stream of rodents filed into my house. I scampered back to the kitchen to whip up more food. Then I dashed around looking for extra plates, cups, and chairs, and a super-long tablecloth.

After we had all stuffed our bellies, Grandfather pounded on the table. "I'd just like to thank Geronimo for hosting this wonderful family reunion. Even though his mashed potatoes were awful and his

AT LAST, WE WERE ALL READY TO EAT.

cheesecake tastes like paste, he's a Stilton and he tried his best," he squeaked.

I chewed my whiskers in a rage. Paste?

I opened my mouth to protest, but Grandfather held up his paw. "No need to thank me, Grandson," he went on. "We Stiltons stick together. Which reminds me, I wanted to tell you all where our family name comes from. There is a little village in England called Stilton. That is where we got our name."

I nodded. Still, that didn't explain why I received that letter from Ratly Von Doright III asking us not to use the name STILTON.

I was more **confused** than ever. Was Stilton a town, a cheese, or a family?

At that moment, the clock struck MIDNIGHT. Ding-dong! Ding-dong!

All members of the Stilton family got up and left. It was late!

I washed the dishes and got ready for bed. But, before I turned off the light, I looked up the word *Stilton* in the encyclopedia.

Drifting off to sleep, I read:

Stilton: an ancient English village. Also the name of a famous cheese . . .

I fell asleep with my snout in the book.

zzz...zzzzzzz...zzz..

GERONIMOOOOOOOO!

I woke with a START and glanced over at the alarm clock. It was half-past five.

What had woken me up?

Just then, I heard it. Someone was ringing my doorbell, calling me on the house phone, and buzzing my cell phone. Plus, a CAR HORN was honking right in front of my mouse hole!

I put my paws over my ears.

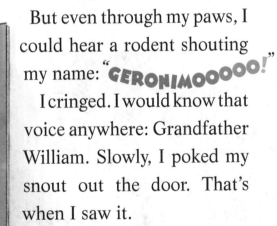

But even through my paws, I could hear a rodent shouting my name: "GERONIMOOOOO!"

I cringed. I would know that voice anywhere: Grandfather William. Slowly, I poked my snout out the door. That's when I saw it.

It was huge.

It was yellow.

Yes, it was Grandfather William's

enormouse cheese-colored camper!

Five rodent heads and ten rodent paws were sticking out of the camper windows. They were all waving *cheerily* at me.

Besides Grandfather William, there was Thea, Trap, Benjamin, and Tina.

"Grandson! What are you doing still in your pajamas?" Grandfather bellowed. "How many times do I have to tell you, morning is the best time to travel? Now shake a paw!"

"Tr-tr-travel?" I stammered. "But I hate to travel. Where are you going?"

Grandfather **GRABBED** me by the ear. "If you had answered your phone, you would know by now. I just called you! We're going to Stilton, England. *NOW HURRY UP*,

Grandson!" he squeaked.

I tried to protest. I had a **million** projects to finish at work. Did I tell you that I am the publisher of *The Rodent's Gazette*? It's the most *famouse* newspaper on Mouse Island. And besides, I hadn't packed.

Of course, Grandfather didn't hear a word I said. Instead, he pulled out a **stopwatch**.

"You have exactly sixty seconds to get ready, Grandson! That's one minute! Now **move** that tail!" he shrieked.

He began counting out loud.

What could I do? No one ever says no to Grandfather William.

I raced around my mouse hole at record speed. I showered so fast the water barely hit my fur. And I only had time to brush three teeth! Oh, how I hate *rushing* around.

"NO TIME TO WASTE!"

1

Shower:
12 seconds!

2

Brushing of teeth:
6 seconds!

3

Combing of
whiskers:
1 second!

4

Getting dressed:
11 seconds!

5

Putting knot in tie:
3 seconds!

6

Grabbing
passport:
9 seconds!

7

Opening suitcase:
1 second!

8

Transferring everything
from the wardrobe to
suitcase: 16 seconds!

9

Closing suitcase:
1 second!

TOTAL: EXACTLY SIXTY SECONDS!

my grandfather shouted, interrupting my thoughts. "Throw some clothes in a bag, and we're out of here!"

SIXTY SECONDS later, I reluctantly stumbled up the steps of the camper.

"What took you so long?" My cousin Trap smirked. Then the camper took off like a rocket.

It was a long journey. We had to travel from Mouse Island all the way across the **Ratlantic Ocean**. We drove the camper onto a ferry. From there, it took many days to reach the coast of England.

If there's one thing I hate more than an airplane, it's a boat. I was seasick the whole time!

Great Britain is the largest island in Europe (80,800 square miles). Geographically, the island is made up of the countries of England, Scotland, and Wales. Politically, Great Britain and Northern Ireland together are called the United Kingdom of Great Britain and Northern Ireland.

Great Britain is separated from mainland Europe by a body of water called the English Channel. The island is connected to mainland Europe by the Chunnel, a 31-mile train tunnel that runs under the water!

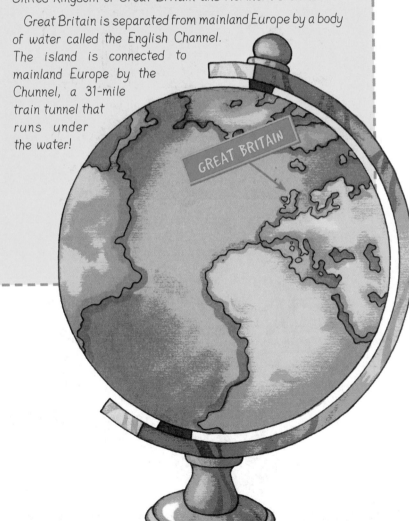

GREAT BRITAIN

GRANDFATHER WILLIAM'S CAMPER

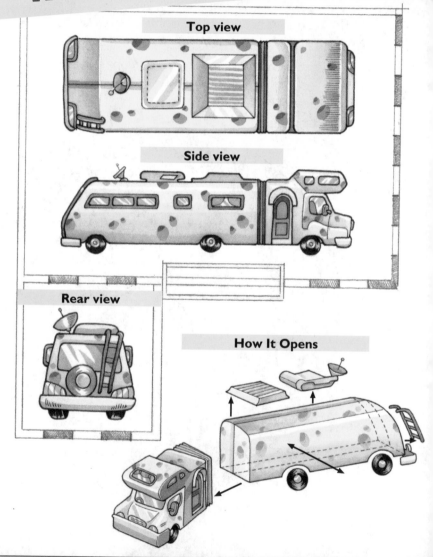

Top view

Side view

Rear view

How It Opens

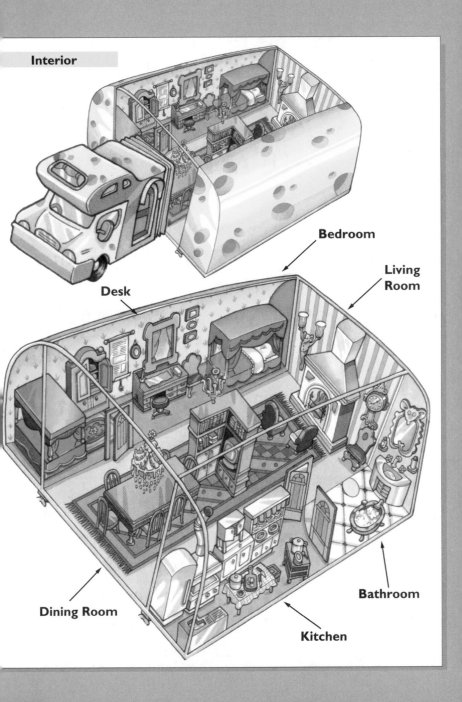

Interior

Bedroom

Living Room

Desk

Dining Room

Kitchen

Bathroom

GRANDFATHER'S CAMPER

At last, we reached England. I was so happy to see land, I jumped off the ferry and kissed the ground.

My sister had to pull me back into the camper. "Really, you're so **embarrassing**, Gerrykins," she scolded. Then Grandfather revved the engine. We took off in a cloud of dust. I noticed a few rodents on the ferry shaking their heads at us. Now *that's* what I call **embarrassing**.

An hour later, we passed a sign. It said YOU ARE ENTERING THE VILLAGE OF STILTON.

We were so excited. Everyone jumped out of the camper and took pictures of the sign. Then we decided to celebrate at a local **restaurant**.

"**I'M STARVING**! In fact, if I don't eat something right now, I'm going to die of hunger!" Trap cried once we got inside the restaurant. He grabbed a waiter and ordered a pound of Stilton cheese.

But the waiter just shook his head. "Very sorry, sir, but we're out of Stilton. A thief broke into our cellar and he ran away with all our Stilton cheese. It's a real mystery."

As soon as he said *mystery*, my sister Thea's ears perked up. She loves to solve mysteries! In a flash, she scampered down to the cellar to take some pictures.

At that moment, an old lady walked past us. She had just filled her plate at the buffet bar.

My cousin's eyes grew wide. His mouth began to water. With a squeak, he reached out and snatched a hunk of cheese from the old lady's plate.

"Sorry, madam, but I must try your cheese. I am a cheeseologist and I am conducting an important experiment," he explained, popping the cheese into his mouth.

Then, paws flying, Trap RACED to the buffet table. He quickly assembled a triple-decker cheese sandwich complete with pickles, lettuce, and sixteen green olives. He devoured the whole thing in one gulp.

"Ahem, the experiment is over!" he announced a few seconds later. "I have decided there is nothing special about that cheese!"

Then he rubbed his tummy and let out a loud BURP.

Did I mention my cousin has zero table manners?

Meanwhile, the old lady was still staring at her empty plate. She looked like she had no idea what had just happened.

"**Who** stole my cheese? **Who** would do such a horrible thing?" she squeaked.

I glared at my cousin. Someone had to apologize for his behavior. I decided it was up to me. After all, I am the gentlemouse in the family. But as I walked toward the old lady, three things happened. First, I *SLIPPED* on a cheese rind. Then I did a triple SOMERSAULT in the air, winding up face down. Finally, I landed $\mathcal{Smack}$ in the middle of the buffet table with a tomato in my mouth.

Immediately, the old lady began hitting me over the head with her umbrella. "How dare you steal my cheese, you **horrible thief**!" she squeaked.

Someone had to apologize!

I slipped on a cheese rind..

...did a triple somersault in the air...

...winding up snout-first...

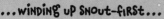

...and landed smack in the middle of the buffet table!

THIEF!

The rodents at the buffet table stared at me in horror.

I tried to explain that it wasn't me, but no one would listen.

I looked around for my cousin, but he was already headed for the door. I followed with my tail between my legs. How humiliating!

"You are so **embarrassing**, Gerry Berry," Trap CHUCKLED as we climbed aboard the camper.

STEAM poured from my ears. Oh, why did these things always happen to me?

DON'T MIND IF I DO!

We decided to go to a supermarket next. Maybe we could find some Stilton cheese there! A few miles down the road, we spotted an **ENORMOUSE** Stop & Squeak. The deli counter was longer than a lane at the Rattown Bowling Alley. They had cheddar. They had Swiss. They had Muenster.

But there wasn't a trace of Stilton.

"A thief stole all of the Stilton cheese from our stockroom," a mouse behind the counter explained. "It's a real mystery."

LIKE A SHOT, Thea snuck off to the stockroom, camera in paw. Did I mention that she loves a good mystery?

Meanwhile, the mouse behind the counter held out a silver plate. It was filled with little cubes of cheese. Each one had a toothpick in it. "Please feel free to sample any of our other cheeses," she offered.

I was about to reach for a cube, when a paw shoved me aside. "Don't mind if I do!" Trap's voice followed. "After all, I am a cheese expert!"

My cousin doesn't really know anything about cheeses. He just likes to eat them! I

HOW DO YOU NIBBLE?
A GUIDE TO THE REAL YOU

SUSPICIOUS: You are extremely picky when it comes to trying new foods. You never trust expiration dates. You bring your own silverware when you go out to eat in a restaurant.

SUPER-ORGANIZED: You eat the same foods on the same days of the week. On Mondays, you have a cheese casserole. On Tuesdays, you have mozzarella meatballs. On Wednesdays, you have cheddar cheese omelets, etc.

WISHY-WASHY: You can never make up your mind when you are ordering food at a restaurant. One day, your favorite cheese is cheddar, the next it's Swiss.

EXCESSIVE: You love to eat anything and everything. You have no idea when enough is enough. All of your dreams involve food.

DELICIOUS!

WHICH ONE OF THOSE IS MINE?

DIZZY: You can never remember what you ordered at a restaurant. Sometimes you confuse breakfasttime and dinnertime.

CHEESE IS VERY GOOD FOR YOU, YOU KNOW...

CHATTERBOX: You love to talk about food even when you are eating!

TIME TO EAT!

SOPHISTICATED: You appreciate all types of yummy foods, but you know not to overeat. You like to cook and you also like to eat healthy foods.

was the one working on an encyclopedia of cheeses, after all.

Trap began gobbling down the little pieces of cheese at *SUPERSONIC* speed. A few seconds later, the plate was empty.

The mouse behind the counter was speechless.

I was speechless *and* hungry. Oh, how did I end up with such an obnoxious cousin?

Encyclopedia of cheeses

ALIVE AND SQUEAKING!

After leaving the giant supermarket, we checked out a small cheese shop.

The owner had the same news. A **mysterious** thief had broken into the supply room and stolen all of the Stilton cheese.

He led us down some stairs to the supply room. It was very cold. Even my whiskers were **freezing**!

"We keep it cold, so the food stays fresh," the owner explained.

I **LOOKED** around. At one end of the room

was a **LONG** conveyor belt. It was covered with crates of different foods: carrots, tomatoes, potatoes, cheeses, and lots more.

I was about to check out the cheese crate when a loud shriek filled the air.

"Putrid cheese puffs! There's a mouse-size spider in that corner!" Trap shouted. He raced for the stairs. On his way, he stomped on my **paw**.

"Yikes!" I squeaked, falling back onto the conveyor belt. It sprang to life. I had accidentally hit the ON switch! Before

I could say *Squeak*, the belt grabbed my tie. I was being strangled to death!

Luckily, my sister Thea came to my rescue. She grabbed a pair of scissors and cut my tie.

That was a close call!

We said good-bye to the store owner and **got back in** the camper. Grandfather did a few doughnuts in the parking lot before we took off. This time, I didn't mind. I was just happy to be alive and squeaking!

YIKES!

History of Stilton Cheese, The King of English Cheeses

Stilton cheese dates back to the beginning of the 1700s. It is only produced in the three counties of Derbyshire, Leicestershire, and Nottinghamshire, England, and is made exclusively with locally produced milk. Only six creameries are authorized to make Stilton, and they produce more than a million blocks of cheese per year! It is made according to a process that has remained the same throughout the centuries.

The cheese takes its name from the English village of Stilton. It was not made in Stilton, but it was sold there. Indeed, Stilton was an important stop for people traveling by coach during the 1700s. Stilton was about a day's journey

from London (eighty miles). While the horses were changed, refreshments were served to the travelers, including some of the blue-veined cheese. And it became more and more famouse!

Even today, Stilton is made by hand according to traditional methods. This is what distinguishes it from all other cheeses. For this reason, Stilton has been granted the status of "protected designation of origin" (PDO). This guarantees that the product is made according to traditional methods. Therefore, Stilton cannot be made in any other part of the world!

This is a ceramic Wedgewood container, designed in the early 1800s. It was used to cover Stilton cheese and keep it from drying out.

STILTON
MAKERS · ASSOC.
CHEESE

The logo of the Stilton Cheesemakers' Association

Special cheese knives were often used to serve Stilton (figures 1 and 2). After 1930, when Stilton cheese became more well-known, a new tool was introduced (figure 3). It had a pointed tip used to slice the cheese more evenly.

I Wish . . .

We headed north to one of the towns where they make Stilton cheese. As we drove, Trap kept everyone entertained by telling stories. Unfortunately, they were **all** about me! He told about the time I got my tail stuck in his refrigerator. He told about the time I hit myself in the head with my own golf club. Then he showed everyone the **embarrassing** T-shirts he wore when we went to Club Mouse last year.

I **gnashed** my teeth. Oh, how I wished I was on vacation now. Away from my cousin!

S . . . AS IN
SHADOW!

I was still stewing over Trap's T-shirts when Thea began squeaking. She was pawing through the photos she had taken so far.

Thea passed the pictures around for everyone to see. "Look, the thief has left his signature in every shot!" she cried.

My sister was right about one thing. The thief had left a mark. But the thief wasn't a "he" — it was a "she."

"It's the mark of the Shadow!" I cried. Everyone in New Mouse City knew about the Shadow. She was a notorious **thief** who was known for her clever disguises.

A while back, I had come snout-to-snout with the Shadow at the Egyptian Mouseum.

Can you find the mark of the Shadow in these photos?

Restaurant

Supermarket

Cheese Shop

I was on one of my many adventures, looking for a SPOOKY mummy with no name. But that's another story!

Now we had to find the Shadow again. But how?

"To **catch** a thief, you have to figure out where he or she will strike next," my grandfather advised.

The room fell silent. We were all deep in thought. Just then, we heard a loud shriek coming from the kitchen. A second later, Trap raced out, followed by a furious Tina Spicytail. She waved her rolling pin in the air. "How dare you lay your paws on my gourmet cheese basket!" she squeaked.

"I was just tasting!" Trap cried. "I am a cheeseologist, after all!"

Tina kept running after my cousin. "Cheeseologists should keep their paws out

of other mice's things!"

Uh-oh. We had all heard about Tina's cheese basket. It was a present from her niece. She had bought it for Tina on a class trip to the Fine Fur Dairy Farm.

That gave me an idea!

If we couldn't find Stilton cheese at the supermarket or the cheese shop, maybe we could find it at a cheese factory!

Doing!!!

WHISKER-LICKIN' GOOD

We found a cheese factory listed on the map and took off again. When we arrived at the factory, the owner gave us a tour. It was fascinating. I decided to take notes. I would use them for my cheese encyclopedia!

First, we all had to wash our paws. Then we had to put on special hats so that our fur did not get into the cheese. I was happy

to see that they were big on hygiene at this factory. Once I bought a piece of cheddar that had a brown strand of fur in the middle of it. **Yuck!** I couldn't look at cheese for a whole week — and that's an awfully long time for a rodent!

We entered a big room. It was very cold. The owner pointed to a **huge** vat full of milk. He showed us how the milk was mixed with other ingredients to make the cheese. Then it was poured into cylinder-shaped molds. When the cheese came out of the molds, it was smoothed by paw and stored on very **LONG** racks. Then, we saw a mouse sticking a long metal rod into the cheese. Poking holes in the cheese made those famous **blue** veins. Then

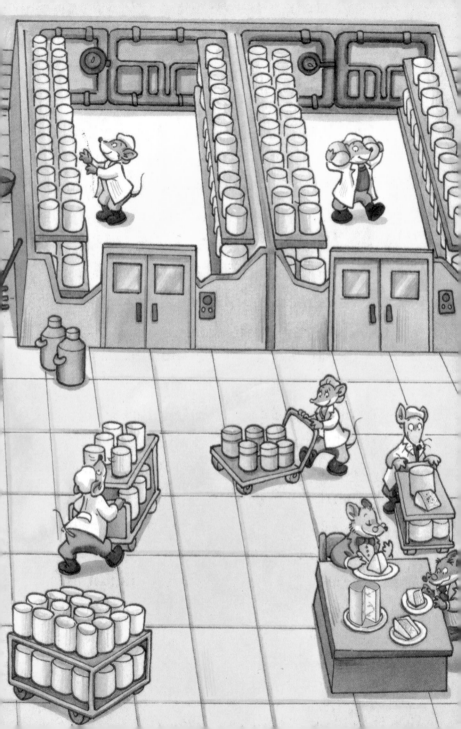

another mouse with **BIG** muscles turned the cheeses over every other day to keep the moisture consistent throughout the aging process. And all this work was done by hand, not machines! Finally, a taster made sure the cheese had aged properly to be good enough to eat.

"Now there's a job I could sink my teeth into!" Trap smirked.

I rolled my **EYES**. Trap? A cheese taster? Now that was a scary idea. Once my cousin had sunk his teeth into a tasty piece of cheese, he'd never stop. He'd **SCARF DOWN** every hunk of cheese in the whole factory. They'd have to close the place. All of the factory rodents would be out of jobs. They'd have no money for food. They might even starve to death! Well, OK, maybe they wouldn't go **PAWS-UP**, but you get the picture. It would be a disaster!

At last, it was time to leave. My whole family headed for the exit. I decided to stay behind to work on my encyclopedia. "Don't hold dinner for me," I squeaked as they walked to the camper. "This **cheese** has put me in the mood to write."

I took a few more notes. But it was so cold, my whiskers were starting to freeze. Maybe writing in a cold cheese factory wasn't such a smart idea after all!

Shivering, I pushed on the doors marked EXIT. Nothing happened. The doors didn't budge. That's when the horrible truth hit me. Some crazy rodent had locked me inside the freezing cold factory!

LIKE A MOUSE
IN A TRAP!

I screamed. I squeaked. I pounded my paws on the heavy metal doors. Yes, mouse friends, I was having a full-blown panic attack.

"Let me out of here!"

I cried.

But nobody answered. They'd all left.

The factory was deserted. I felt like a rat caught in a trap. And not just any trap. A trap in the middle of the **ARCTIC**!

I looked at the thermometer. It read twenty degrees below zero! Holey cheese!

If I didn't get out of this place soon, I'd turn into a mousicle for sure. Headlines flashed before my eyes: STILTON FOUND FROZEN IN FACTORY! PUBLISHER PERISHES ON TOP OF COLD CHEESE MOLD!

SUDDENLY, I heard a muffled sound.

Someone was drilling a hole in the wall. Yikes! Who was breaking into the factory? A shiver ran down my spine. And this time it wasn't because of the cold.

Just then, a FLASHLIGHT peeked through the hole in the wall.

I hid behind a rack of cheese, trembling with fear. I wanted to run. I wanted to hide. I wanted my mommy!

A SHADOW
IN THE DARK

From the hole in the wall, the shadow of a rodent all in black popped out.

It was very thin and very agile.

It was wearing a mask that covered its whole face. All I could make out was a pair of icy blue eyes that glowed in the dark.

Hmmm. Where had I seen eyes like that before?

The mysterious rodent looked around. I gulped. Did it see me? I closed my eyes. I practiced sending a message with my mind. I had seen a mouse do it once on TV.

First, I concentrated really hard. Then I thought, *Move along. Nothing to see here.*

It worked! The intruder **turned away** from me. I was thrilled. Maybe I had discovered my new calling. Maybe I could read minds, too! I could be one pawstep away from fame! Fortune! Free cheese from adoring fans!

I was so excited, I practically squeaked. Then I remembered where I was. I looked up. The mysterious mouse was hard at work loading cheese into a wheelbarrow.

Then it put the cheese through the hole in the wall.

After cleaning out all the cheese in the **FACTORY**, the rodent left its signature on the wall. Ah-ha! I should have known. It was the mark of the Shadow!

So we meet again, I thought. Oops. I hoped the Shadow didn't hear my thoughts this time. I didn't want her to know I was **following** her.

This mind-message thing was a little tricky. But there was no time to worry about that now. I had to keep my eyes on the Shadow.

I watched as she climbed back through the hole in the wall. I scurried to peek through the hole as she loaded the cheese onto a truck outside. I was OUTRAGED. How dare the Shadow steal all of the Stilton cheese from that nice factory owner!

I was **scared** out of my fur. But I had to do something. When the truck roared to life, I quickly scampered outside and hopped on the back. I had no idea where we were headed, but I couldn't turn back now. I had to solve the mystery of the missing cheese. I mean, what could one mouse be doing with all of that Stilton?

Then a horrible thought occurred to me. What if I couldn't find my way back? My family would be worried sick. They'd be **crushed**. They'd be devastated. They'd search for me for twenty years. Well, OK, maybe more like twenty minutes, but I bet they'd at least miss dinner.

That's when I came up with a PLAN. I'd leave a trail behind me, just like Hansel and Gretelmouse. But instead of bread crumbs, I'd roll some cheese off the back of the truck. Then my family could find me for sure. They'd just have to follow the cheese trail!

The truck rumbled past snow-covered hills. The road got steeper and steeper, and I continued to leave a trail behind us.

Finally, at midnight, we stopped. I shivered.

We were here. But **WHERE** *was* here?

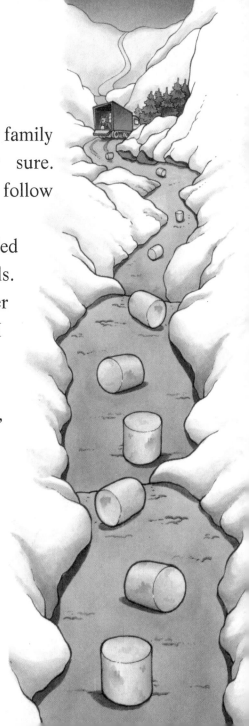

SNOW, SNOW, AND MORE SNOW!

As soon as we rolled to a stop, there was silence.

I jumped off the **TRUCK** and hid behind a PILE of snow. I looked around me. All I could see was snow, snow, and more snow!

Ice-covered trees cast scary **shadows** on the ground. I twisted my tail up in knots. Oh, why had I jumped on that truck? I could have been home safe and sound, warming my paws by the fire. Well, OK, I wouldn't really be at home. I'd be in Grandfather's camper. And I'd probably be arguing with my cousin. But at least I wouldn't be stuck in the middle of these strange woods, **freezing my tail off**!

I shivered. I was so cold I could barely wiggle my paws.

Not the Shadow. She **SPRANG** from the truck like a jackrat in the box. Then she began unloading the cheese. I hoped she wouldn't notice that some was missing!

I didn't have much time to think about it, though. When she finished, she took off into the woods.

Yikes!

I followed her quietly down a long, winding path, past a small stream, and up a hill.

Snow-covered pine trees loomed all around me. The wind WHiSPERED AND MOANED. I was shaking in my fur. Did I mention I'm a bit of a 'fraidy mouse?

At last, I spotted a **strange-looking** house. I cleaned my glasses to see better. Could it be?

Yes, it was! It was a whole house built out of cheese. Stilton cheese, to be exact!

The walls were made with cheese bricks. The roof was covered with cheese rinds. What a sight!

I broke off a tiny piece of the house and tasted it.

Yum! It was whisker-licking good!

I watched as the thief headed through the front door. I tried peeking through the window, but it was no use. The Shadow had pulled the curtains shut. Rats! There was only one thing left to do. Without a sound, I slipped through the front door behind the Shadow.

The place was *incredible*. Everything was

made out of cheese! There was a cheese sofa, a cheese TV, a cheese computer, and even a SWIMMING POOL filled with melted cheese!

FIT TO BE QUEEN!

At that very moment, the Shadow strolled into the room.

I hid behind a column and watched as she **QUICKLY** removed her black hood. A mass of blonde hair cascaded down her back.

I sighed. Too bad the Shadow was a thief. She really was one very attractive rodent.

Just then, she whipped out her cell phone and punched in a number.

"It's the **Shadow**. Everything is fine. Tonight I hit every Stilton cheese factory. Now all of England's Stilton is under my **CONTROL**!" she chuckled.

I could hear someone snickering on the other end of the phone. I wondered who she was squeaking to.

The Shadow continued excitedly, clapping her paws in delight. "I've always *dreamed* of having a house made of **cheese** inside and out! And with this new load of cheese, I can **FINALLY** finish the job. I can't believe I stole all of the Stilton cheese in England! Of course, you know I had to have Stilton. It is the *king* of cheeses!" She giggled.

"And I always say, I am fit to be queen! After all, I'm the perfect package: *beautiful* and **smart**. My dear cousin, now you can be the first to publish news of the cheese thief in your newspaper in New Mouse City!"

I was shocked.

A newspaper? On Mouse Island? Who was the Shadow squeaking to?

Do You Like My House?

Without thinking, I let out a squeak of SURPRISE.

The thief was beside me in no time. Uh-oh. *She smiled charmingly*. Her blue eyes glittered like ice.

"So, we meet again, Geronimo Stilton." She grinned. "Do you like my house? Only *I* could afford such a thing. A house made of cheese is every mouse's dream. Don't you agree?" she cooed.

I frowned. Who would want to live in a house built out of STOLEN cheese?

"Well, it's not *my* dream," I squeaked.

The Shadow just shrugged. "Oh, who cares what you think, anyway?" She snickered.

"The most important thing is that now I have everything I want. A fabumouse house, a nice car, expensive clothes. I'M RICH, RICH, RICH! What more could a mouse want?"

I shook my head. How sad. The Shadow had no idea what she was missing out on. I mean, it's fabumouse to have nice things, but what about friends and family? Weren't they important, too?

"Um, well, money is nice . . . Shadow," I began. "But wouldn't it be nicer if you had some friends to share all your cheese with? And what about the needy rodents in the world? Wouldn't it be great if you could use some of your money to feed an orphanage of hungry mice?"

The Shadow smiled beneath her whiskers. "Oh, *Geronimo Stilton*. You are such a sap. Always doing good things for others. No wonder my cherished cousin Sally Ratmousen can't stand you." She smirked.

Steam poured from my ears. That's who the Shadow had been on the phone with! Just hearing Sally Ratmousen's name got my blood boiling. She was the owner of *The Daily Rat,* and my number one enemy. Sally

Sally Ratmousen

was always playing rotten tricks on me. One time, she dusted itching powder on every single copy of *The Rodent's Gazette*. Mice were scratching their fur for weeks! Another time, she sent a package of rancid cheese to my mouse hole at 8 Mouseford Lane. It smelled so bad, I could hardly breathe.

Yes, Sally Ratmousen was one **rotten** mouse. It just figures that she was related to a thief!

What had I gotten myself into? At least I'd left an escape trail. . . .

MY OWN PRIVATE HIDEOUT

"So, *Geronimo*," the Shadow said with a smirk. "Too bad you're such a careless snoop. Now you're stuck up here forever. I mean, no one will ever find this place. No one knows it exists. It's my own private hideout!" She cackled with glee. "Yep, Stilton, you might as well **KISS** your little newspaper good-bye. In fact, I think I'll call my cousin and tell her the great news."

I chewed my whiskers. I was getting sick and tired of the Shadow and her **KNOW-IT-ALL** attitude. Before I could stop myself, I spilled the beans about my *Hansel and Gretelmouse* plan. I told her about leaving the trail of cheese behind. "In fact, my family should be here any minute. And you'll go straight to jail," I finished TRIUMPHANTLY.

The Shadow's fur went white. I could tell she was worried. And I was glad! Maybe next time, she'd think before she stole another hunk of cheese.

But then, I noticed a gleam in her eyes.

She plopped down next to me on the couch.

"So tell me about your *family*, Geronimo," she cooed. "Are they all as *handsome* as you?"

I blushed. "Well, I, er, um . . ." I stammered.

She patted my sleeve. "Did anyone ever tell you that you are a wonderful *dresser*? Where did you find this beautiful red tie? And your jacket is so *SHARP*," she squeaked.

er, um...

er, um...

By now, I was as *red* as the nose on Rudolph, the Red-Nosed Rodent. I mean, even though the Shadow was a thief, I was still **flattered**.

Soon we were gabbing away like old friends. We talked about books, movies, and music. I was surprised. I mean, besides the stealing, the Shadow seemed like a very smart rodent.

I told her all about *The Rodent's Gazette*. I even told her about the encyclopedia of

er, um...

cheeses I was writing.

Just thinking about cheese made my tummy RUMBLE. The Shadow kindly brought out a platter of Stilton. I felt bad about eating the stolen cheese, but what could I do? I was starving.

Eating all of that cheese made me sleepy!

"Why don't you close your eyes? Put your **PaWS** up," the Shadow suggested with a smile.

I was feeling so relaxed. So tired. Part of my brain told me not to do it. After all, the Shadow was a wanted criminal. But the other part of me said go ahead. I mean, what harm could a quick mouse nap do?

I was just drifting off when it hit me. No, not another idea. A hammer. Yes, the Shadow had hidden a **gigundo hammer** under the couch cushion! She clocked me over the snout with it.

"CHEWY CHEESE STICKS!" I managed to cry. Then I was down for the count.

She clocked me over the snout!

DON'T BE SUCH A 'FRAIDY MOUSE!

I woke up when a pail of **icy cold water** hit me in the snout.

My eyes **POPPED** open. A slimy **WHITE** ghost stood in front of me. He had a strangely familiar expression on his face.

"**Rat-munching rattlesnakes!**" I shrieked.

The ghost rolled its eyes. "Don't be such a 'fraidy mouse, Germeister," it scoffed.

Now I knew why the ghost looked so familiar. It was my cousin Trap!

He had fallen into the Shadow's indoor swimming pool. Trap was covered from head to tail with melted cheese!

"Mozzarella," he said, licking his whiskers. Then he waved his tail. Cheese splattered all over me. "Go ahead! Try some, Gerry Berry." Trap chuckled. "It's delicious."

I looked down at my favorite suit. It was a mess. Too bad I had just had it dry-cleaned.

I was about to SCREAM at Trap when I felt two tiny paws around my waist. It was my dear, sweet nephew, Benjamin.

"Oh, Uncle, you were so smart to LEAVE that trail of cheese behind. We were so worried about you!" he squeaked.

I gave my nephew a warm hug. Then I told my family about the **Shadow**. I explained how she had stolen all of the Stilton cheese in England. And I told them how she had built this dream house out of cheese.

When I was finished, I looked around. My whole family stood in front of me. But I realized someone was missing. Where was the Shadow?

"We have to find her," I squeaked.

My sister nodded. "That **BLONDE** thief needs to go to jail," she insisted.

I tried to picture the Shadow behind bars, but for some reason I couldn't. She was so pretty and smart. She didn't seem like the kind of rodent who belonged in the slammer.

"You know, she really is a very **fascinating** mouse," I said dreamily. "Maybe we should think about it before

we turn her in. She's not such a bad rodent when you get to know her. Besides, she said I was handsome."

My sister rolled her eyes. "Oh, little brother," she snickered. "How could you fall for that sneaky thief?"

I blushed. I knew it was wrong to like a thief, but I couldn't help it. The Shadow was so charming. Plus, no mouse had ever told me they liked the way I dressed before. Then again, no mouse had ever hit me over the head with a hammer before, either.

I was still thinking about the Shadow when Trap pulled a fork out of his pocket. "Well, there is one thing you've gotta love about the Shadow," he grinned. "You've gotta love her house."

Then, with a squeak, he stuck his fork into the coffee table and started to eat it. YUM!

You've gotta love a house of cheese—yum!

THE SHADOW'S TRICKS

We had to find the **Shadow**. But where could she be?

First, we searched inside the house. She was **NOWHERE** in sight. Then we headed outside. It wasn't easy. We had to drag Trap out of the house. He was busy taste-testing the delicious cheese wallpaper!

Lucky for us, the Shadow's pawprints stood out in the snow. But she was sneaky. At one point, she covered her tracks with a twig. She walked backward, so her footprints were pointing the wrong way.

Then she even walked in an icy stream so we would lose track of her.

But we kept going.

I wasn't about to let the Shadow trick me again! I, *Geronimo Stilton*, had learned my lesson . . . even if she was awfully pretty. And smart. And . . .

Finally, we came to a giant supermarket. It was packed with rodents. There was no way we would ever find the Shadow here. It was a lost cause!

But then, among the crowds, I spotted her!

She saw me, too. I tried to reach her, but it was useless. She waved good-bye, then slipped away.

THE SHADOW

Oh, well. I guess becoming friends with a thief wasn't such a good idea, anyway.

LONG LIVE THE STILTON FAMILY!

Even though the Shadow got away, we had at least found all of the **stolen** cheese.

We went back to the cheese house and loaded everything onto the **Shadow's** truck. Then we returned it to the **cheese** factory, where it belonged.

We were treated like heroes. They even threw a special party for us inside the factory!

It was a little cold, but how could I complain? The president of the Stilton Cheesemakers' Association even made a speech.

"Geronimo, thanks to you, we have solved this terrible crime. How can we ever repay you?" he said.

I **straightened** my tie. "Well, um, there is one thing you could do for me. I would like to be able to call myself Stilton. I'm very attached to my name," I explained.

The president nodded. A chorus of voices followed. "**Long live the Stilton family! Long live Geronimo Stilton!**" they squeaked.

Out of the corner of my eye, I saw that my cousin was turning green with envy.

"I don't know why they're making such a big deal over Geronimo," he muttered, sulking.

I pretended I didn't hear him.

How Could You Be So Rude?

It was time to go home. All of the factory workers returned to their jobs. I said goodbye and headed for the door. But just then, Trap **STUCK OUT** his paw. I tripped. **Splat!** I fell **SNOUT-FIRST** into a vat of milk.

GLb... GLbbb... bLubbb...

I fell SNOUT-FIRST iNto a vat of MiLK.

TRap Stuck out His paw.

The owner of the cheese factory rushed over. "What is the meaning of this, Mr. Stilton? We do not allow swimming in our milk vats! What about **hygiene**?" he scolded me.

I tried to explain, but my cousin interrupted me. "Oh, Germeister, how could you be so rude?" He smirked, leaning back on a rack of cheese.

THE RACK TOPPLED OVER.

Crash! The rack toppled over, crashing into another rack, and another. It was like watching a game of cheese dominoes.

CHEESE WAS ROLLING EVERYWHERE!

Cheeses shaped like giant marshmallows **were rolling** everywhere.

Workers rushed to the rescue. "You're making a mess!" they yelled at me.

I tried to explain, but my cousin interrupted me again. "Oh, Gerry Berry, **YOU REALLY SHOULD BE MORE CAREFUL**," he snorted.

Trap got his paws on a cheese drill.

A second later, he got his paws on a cheese drill. He began drilling right and left into the cheeses like a mad mouse. **"Yum! Yum!"** he cried, tasting as many as he could. I tried to stop him. Just as I tore the drill from his paws, the taster arrived.

He shot me a **STERN** look. "No one touches my cheese drill," he declared. "Mr. Stilton, I would have expected you to know better! You're a grown mouse!"

I tore the DRILL from his paws.

My snout turned bright **red**. I tried to explain, but my cousin shook his head. "Oh, Gerrykins, when will you ever admit to your mistakes?" He snickered.

That was it. I had had enough. I was sick of my cousin and his jealous behavior. I was tired of his embarrassing tricks. He was the one acting like a spoiled mouselet, and I was the one getting in trouble!

I started yelling at Trap. He yelled back. We yelled and screamed at each other for so long we almost lost our squeaks. Back and forth, back and forth, back and forth.

Then Trap said, **"I NEVER WANT TO SEE YOU AGAIN!"** **"Fine with me!"** I agreed.

I couldn't stand another minute with
my cousin. I took a plane back to
Mouse Island right away.
Trap went by boat. And the
rest of my family rode on
the ferry, in the camper.
I couldn't wait to get
home to my comfy
mouse hole, and far, far
away from my cousin!

ONE LOUD, OBNOXIOUS, ANNOYING THING

A *week* passed.

Then two. Then three.

I thought for sure my cousin would stop by. But he didn't.

Oh, well. I was too **BUSY** to worry about it. Christmas was just around the corner. I

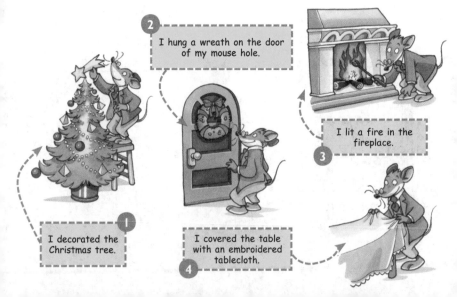

1 I decorated the Christmas tree.

2 I hung a wreath on the door of my mouse hole.

3 I lit a fire in the fireplace.

4 I covered the table with an embroidered tablecloth.

decorated my house for the holidays. I put up my tree. I hung my wreath. I lit candles. Oh, how I **love** the holidays!

On Christmas Eve, the doorbell rang. My relatives came in one by one, loaded down with presents. They crowded into my kitchen. They took over my living room.

Yes, it was a typical Christmas Eve at my house. Well, **except for one thing**. One loud, obnoxious, annoying thing. That's right, my cousin Trap was missing.

5 I put the Christmas centerpiece Benjamin made in the middle of the table.

6 I set the table, using my best dishes.

7 I lit the candles.

8 Then my relatives arrived!

Stilton Tagliatelle

Makes 4 servings

Ingredients

4 quarts water
1 cup tagliatelle pasta
½ cup crumbled Stilton cheese
1 cup sour cream
1 egg, lightly beaten
A dash of pepper, to taste
4 fresh, flat leaf parsley sprigs

Instructions

Make sure to ask an adult for help near the stove!

1. Using a 5- or 6-quart saucepan, bring 4 quarts of water to a boil over medium-high heat. Cover the pan so the water boils quickly. Add salt to the boiling water, then pasta. Cook, uncovered, stirring frequently to keep the pasta from sticking to the sides of the pan. It will take 10 to 14 minutes to cook. Drain thoroughly.

2. Toss cooked pasta with the Stilton, sour cream, beaten egg and pepper. Mix well over low heat, until the egg is cooked through and the Stilton has melted into the pasta. Serve immediately in a casserole dish, garnished with sprigs of parsley.

Stilton Potato Wedges

Makes 4 servings

Ingredients

2 8-ounce potatoes, scrubbed and washed
½ cup fresh white bread crumbs
⅓ cup Blue Stilton cheese, grated
1 egg, beaten
¼ cup butter, melted

Instructions

Make sure to ask an adult for help near the stove!

1. Preheat the oven to 350° Fahrenheit.

2. Cut each potato lengthwise into 8 wedge-shaped pieces of equal size.

3. Microwave the potato wedges on a paper towel for 3 to 5 minutes, until just cooked.

4. Combine the bread crumbs and grated Stilton cheese in a mixing bowl.

5. Dip each potato wedge into the beaten egg, then into the bread crumb mixture. The bread crumb mixture will stick to the egg! Place the wedges on their backs in a roasting tray.

6. Place the roasting tray in the oven and cook for 15 to 20 minutes, until the potato wedges are crisp and brown.

Served as a light meal with salsa and green salad, or as a side dish.

(Recipes courtesy of the Stilton Cheesemakers' Association)

I thought about all of the pranks my cousin had played on me throughout the year. Then I thought about all of the nice things he had done for me. Yes, my cousin could be a royal pain in the fur. But he was still family. I decided to go get him.

"**I'll be right back!**" I told my relatives. Then I headed out into the freezing cold night.

No Sign of Him

I raced over to my cousin's mouse hole. It was locked up tight. I glanced at my watch. It was nine o'clock in the evening. How strange.

Where would my cousin be at this time of night?

He was missing his favorite television show, *Judge Squeaky*.

I walked into the center of town. I looked for him in the stores, the restaurants, and even at the Grand Squeak Cinema. A double feature was playing. *Frankencat II* and *III*. Trap loved *Frankencat I*. We had seen it together. It scared me so badly I had to sleep with the LIGHTS on for a week. Of course, my cousin never let me forget it.

I glanced at my watch again. It was already

ten o'clock.

I was getting worried. **Where could my cousin be at this hour?** He should have been home fixing himself his favorite late-night snack: a double-decker cream cheese sandwich with all the fixings.

I **CHECKED OUT** Squeak and Brew, Lucky Paw Lanes, and Burt and Squeaker's. I traipsed all over town in the snow. But there was **NO SIGN** of him.

By now, it was eleven o'clock.

I was feeling sad and lonely. Everyone was rushing home to be with their families on Christmas. But how could I celebrate Christmas without Trap?

Yes, sometimes he pulled on my whiskers. Yes, sometimes he stepped on my tail. And oh, yes, one time he even pushed me in front

of a moving subway train. But that's another story.

Still, Trap was my cousin. And

I loved him dearly.

I decided if I ever saw him again, I would tell him just that.

I took one last look up and down the streets. I dug through the **snow**. I turned over a few benches. Then I gave up. What else could I do? With a **heavy** heart, I trudged back home.

WHERE HAVE YOU BEEN?

At half-past eleven, I reached Mouseford Lane.

I sighed. Then I slowly climbed up the stairs to my house. **I FELT AWFUL**. What would I tell my relatives? That my cousin had disappeared from the face of the earth, never to be found again?

But just then, the most amazing thing happened. The door opened and a familiar face peeked out. Can you guess who it was?

That's right! It

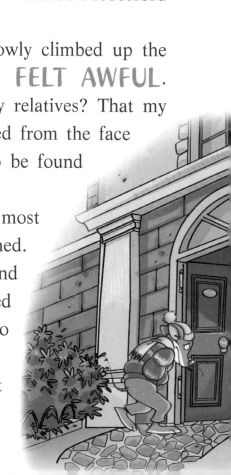

was my loud, obnoxious, annoying, but still lovable *cousin Trap*.

"What's shakin', Cuzinkins? Where have you been? You're missing your own party!" he squeaked.

I giggled. Then I chuckled. Then I rolled on the ground with laughter. I had never been so happy to see a rodent in all my life.

And where had my cousin been on this icy cold Christmas Eve? He had been out searching for yours truly!

"I searched the bookstore, the library, and I even set paw in the mouseum," he said. "And you know, Gerry Berry, you're right. Mouseums aren't totally boring places. This one had a yummy snack shop."

I shook my head. Some things never change.

I hugged my cousin tightly. We both said we were sorry. We promised to try not to fight anymore. Or at least to keep the whisker pulling and tail twisting to a minimum.

Then we exchanged presents. I gave Trap a genuine *solid silver fork*. On the handle was engraved:

TO THE BEST CHEESE-TASTER IN NEW MOUSE CITY
WITH LOVE FROM YOUR COUSIN, GERONIMO

Then he gave me his present. It was a white T-shirt with red lettering. It said, **I'M A STILTON AND PROUD OF IT!**

When Trap took off his jacket, he was wearing the *same* shirt. I grinned.

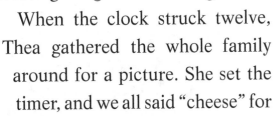

When the clock struck twelve, Thea gathered the whole family around for a picture. She set the timer, and we all said "cheese" for the camera. "Stilton cheese," to be exact.

It was a great shot. But of course, I knew it would be. After all, there is no family like the Stilton family!

there is no family like the Stilton family!

Want to read my next adventure?
It's sure to be a fur-raising experience!

VALLEY OF THE GIANT SKELETONS

Rat-munching rattlesnakes — how do I get myself into these situations? This time, my family swept me off on an adventure to the Gobi Desert in Mongolia. The desert was full of sandstorms and camels and . . . dinosaur bones? I, Geronimo Stilton, am not a big mouse. And these dinosaurs were anything but small! Who knew what could happen next?

ABOUT THE AUTHOR

Born in New Mouse City, Mouse Island, Geronimo Stilton is Rattus Emeritus of Mousomorphic Literature and of Neo-Ratonic Comparative Philosophy. For the past twenty years, he has been running *The Rodent's Gazette*, New Mouse City's most widely read daily newspaper.

Stilton was awarded the Ratitzer Prize for his scoops on *The Curse of the Cheese Pyramid* and *The Search for Sunken Treasure*. He has also received the Andersen 2000 Prize for Personality of the Year. One of his bestsellers won the 2002 eBook Award for world's best ratlings' electronic book. His works have been published all over the globe.

In his spare time, Mr. Stilton collects antique cheese rinds and plays golf. But what he most enjoys is telling stories to his nephew Benjamin.

THE RODENT'S GAZETTE

1. **Main entrance**
2. **Printing presses (where the books and newspaper are printed)**
3. **Accounts department**
4. **Editorial room (where the editors, illustrators, and designers work)**
5. **Geronimo Stilton's office**
6. **Storage space for Geronimo's books**

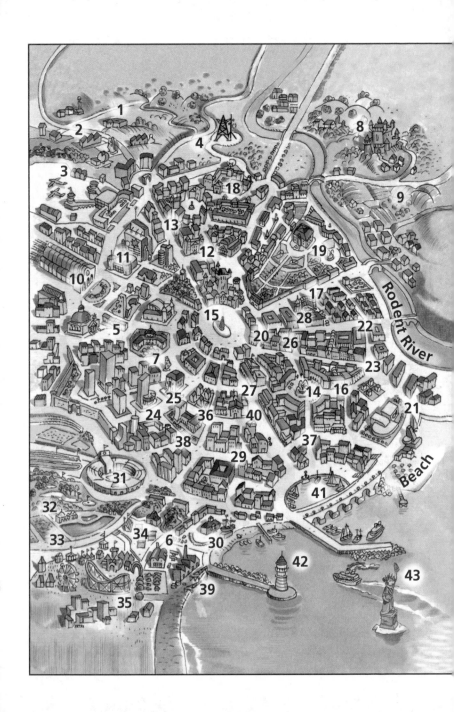

Map of New Mouse City

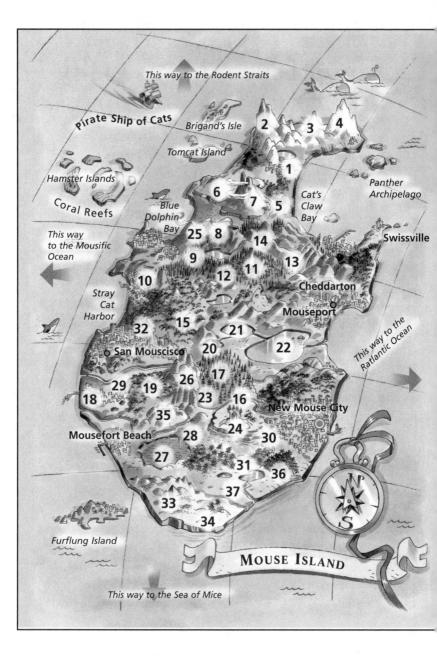

Map of Mouse Island

1. Big Ice Lake
2. Frozen Fur Peak
3. Slipperyslopes Glacier
4. Coldcreeps Peak
5. Ratzikistan
6. Transratania
7. Mount Vamp
8. Roastedrat Volcano
9. Brimstone Lake
10. Poopedcat Pass
11. Stinko Peak
12. Dark Forest
13. Vain Vampires Valley
14. Goose Bumps Gorge
15. The Shadow Line Pass
16. Penny Pincher Castle
17. Nature Reserve Park
18. Las Ratayas Marinas
19. Fossil Forest
20. Lake Lake
21. Lake Lakelake
22. Lake Lakelakelake
23. Cheddar Crag
24. Cannycat Castle
25. Valley of the Giant Sequoia
26. Cheddar Springs
27. Sulfurous Swamp
28. Old Reliable Geyser
29. Vole Vale
30. Ravingrat Ravine
31. Gnat Marshes
32. Munster Highlands
33. Mousehara Desert
34. Oasis of the Sweaty Camel
35. Cabbagehead Hill
36. Rattytrap Jungle
37. Rio Mosquito

#1 Lost Treasure of the Emerald Eye

#2 The Curse of the Cheese Pyramid

#3 Cat and Mouse in a Haunted House

#4 I'm Too Fond of My Fur!

#5 Four Mice Deep in the Jungle

#6 Paws Off, Cheddarface!

#7 Red Pizzas for a Blue Count

#8 Attack of the Bandit Cats

#9 A Fabumouse Vacation for Geronimo

#10 All Because of a Cup of Coffee

#11 It's Halloween, You 'Fraidy Mouse!

#12 Merry Christmas, Geronimo!

#13 The Phantom of the Subway

#14 The Temple of the Ruby of Fire

#15 The Mona Mousa Code

#16 A Cheese-Colored Camper

17 Watch Your hiskers, Stilton!

#18 Shipwreck on the Pirate Islands

#19 My Name Is Stilton, Geronimo Stilton

#20 Surf's Up, Geronimo!

#21 The Wild, Wild West

#22 The Secret of Cacklefur Castle

A Christmas Tale

#23 Valentine's Day Disaster

24 Field Trip to Niagara Falls

#25 The Search for Sunken Treasure

#26 The Mummy with No Name

#27 The Christmas Toy Factory

#28 Wedding Crasher

#29 Down and Out Down Under

#30 The Mouse Island Marathon

and coming soon

#32 Valley of the Giant Skeletons

Dear mouse friends,
Thanks for reading, and farewell
till the next book.
It'll be another whisker-licking-good
adventure, and that's a promise!

Geronimo Stilton